All Hallows Eve

The Story of the Halloween Fairy

Positive Spin Press
Rhode Island, U.S.A.

For You!

© 2006 Lisa Johnson
Illustrations © 2006 Tucker Johnson

ISBN: 0-9773096-1-4

Published by Positive Spin Press   Distributed by Independent Publishers Group
www.positivespinpress.com   www.ipgbook.com   1-800-888-4741

Printed in China

Ever since
Once upon a
time...

...there has been
a little fairy named

Eve!

Eve is a fairy of very small size
    With a warm, sunny smile and dark, friendly eyes

With her wand she can make the most wonderful toys
    They're small and they're fun and she does it with poise

Eve lives in a fairy glen – most fairies do
But this special glen has a pumpkin patch, too!

The fairies carve shapes out to make cozy spaces
That twinkle and sparkle like warm, friendly faces

$\mathscr{F}$or miles around there, most everyone knows
This part of the fairy glen's called *"All Hallows"*

Now, pumpkins and fairies are really quite dandy
But Eve's favorite thing in the whole world is

Candy !!!

She loves it, she loves it, she loves it a bunch
She'd eat it for breakfast, for dinner and lunch!

Now fairies can do that without getting sick
But making the candy – well, that's a big trick!

Try as she may, Eve just couldn't make any
Not even the candy you get for a penny

"Oh, what good is magic," she asked her dear pappy
"If you can't conjure things that will make you most happy?"

Well, Eve found out in the most magical way
One crisp autumn night – that was her Birthday!

Eve called all her friends to come by for some fun
The month was October, the day, thirty-one!

Her party was wonderful, full of fun games
Singing and dancing 'round fairy-sized flames

Now, Eve's favorite game is to play make-believe
And fairies turn into the things they conceive!

...a dragon, a monkey, a princess and knight
A silly old ghost and a witch with a kite

...a lion, a tiger, and there, in the back
Is Eve's favorite friend, a young pirate named Jack

When it was just about time for the cake
A tall birthday tower, Eve wanted to make

She hoped that some fairy dust sprinkled just right
And some fresh Birthday magic would help her this night!

But try as she may, once again Eve was sad –

Just toys *shaped* like candy but tasting quite bad...

A *whistle*
that looked like
a striped *candy cane*

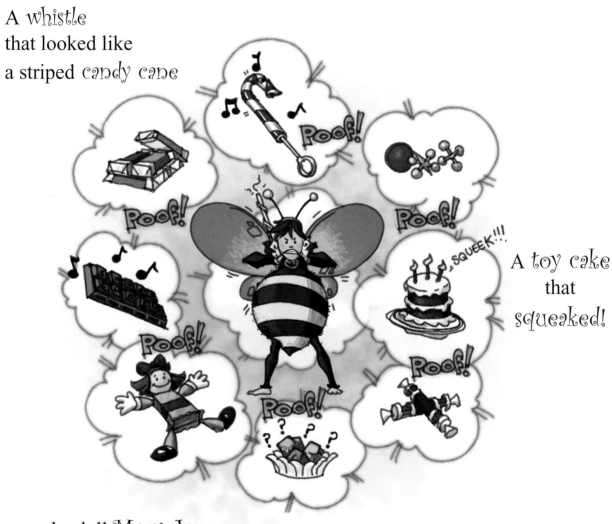

A *toy cake*
that
squeaked!

and a doll *Mary Jane*...

...*Tootsie roll Lincoln logs*

...*candy bar blocks*

Harmonicas, jacks, and a small bowl of rocks...

Her friends, wanting Eve to feel oh-so-much better
    Decided to think up a way that would let her

And Jack, who enjoyed a good puzzle to solve
    Came up with a plan, and he said with resolve

"It's her birthday today, we could help her to smile
    We could get her some treats, a whole sack, a big pile!

We'll let others know that she's so sad without it
    We'll go to each home in the patch, howabout it?"

The others agreed, and set off with a run
    To each home in All Hallows – and boy, it was fun!

Still looking like fanciful, whimsical creatures
    They went off in twos – fairytale double features

They could tell who was home for their pumpkins did shine
And they went to each house and repeated these lines:

"We've come to get All Hallows Eve a nice treat
We're looking for candy and sweet things to eat!

Today is her birthday – we all feel so bad
For she cannot make candy and that makes her sad!"

Sweet candies, confections of all shapes and sizes…
Each fairy home offered them like they were prizes!

At one home, a fairy so funny and quick
Didn't have any candy, so taught Jack a trick!

"Show this trick to Eve and you'll see her bright smile
She'll giggle with laughter at least for a while!"

So well into darkness the fairies collected
   Some treats and a trick that were somehow connected

And finally, (their wings were exhausted, you see)
   They went back to Eve and they cried happily:

"Happy Birthday dear Eve!
We have got a surprise!

Now take a deep breath and please cover your eyes!"

When she opened her eyes, there was candy galore!
Her heart leapt with joy, she had never seen more!

"Oh! Thank you! Oh, thank you! My dream has come true!
And all through the magic of friendship – from you!"

And for Eve, to whom Candy is Wonderful Stuff
Finally, at last, she had quite enough!

Then, Eve remembered the toys she had made!
    She could give them to all of her friends, as a trade!

This made her heart leap again, swelling with joy
    As she handed each fairy a shiny new toy!

Then, Jack did his trick and it turned out just right!
Eve laughed and she laughed, and the whole room was bright!

"Oh, Jack! You're a lantern!" said Eve, "and what's more
You're the best friend a fairy could ever wish for!"

And that, my dear friends, was the first Halloween
But it wasn't the last – and there's lots in between

Each year, on Eve's birthday, the fairies still meet
They dress up, play games, and then beg, "Trick or Treat!"

They give candy to Eve, and she makes each a toy
They celebrate friendship – true Halloween joy!

Oh the fun that they have! Well now, you can join too!
So dress up, go collecting – you know what to do!

Give her your candy – a toy you'll receive!

Share in the magic of All Hallows Eve!

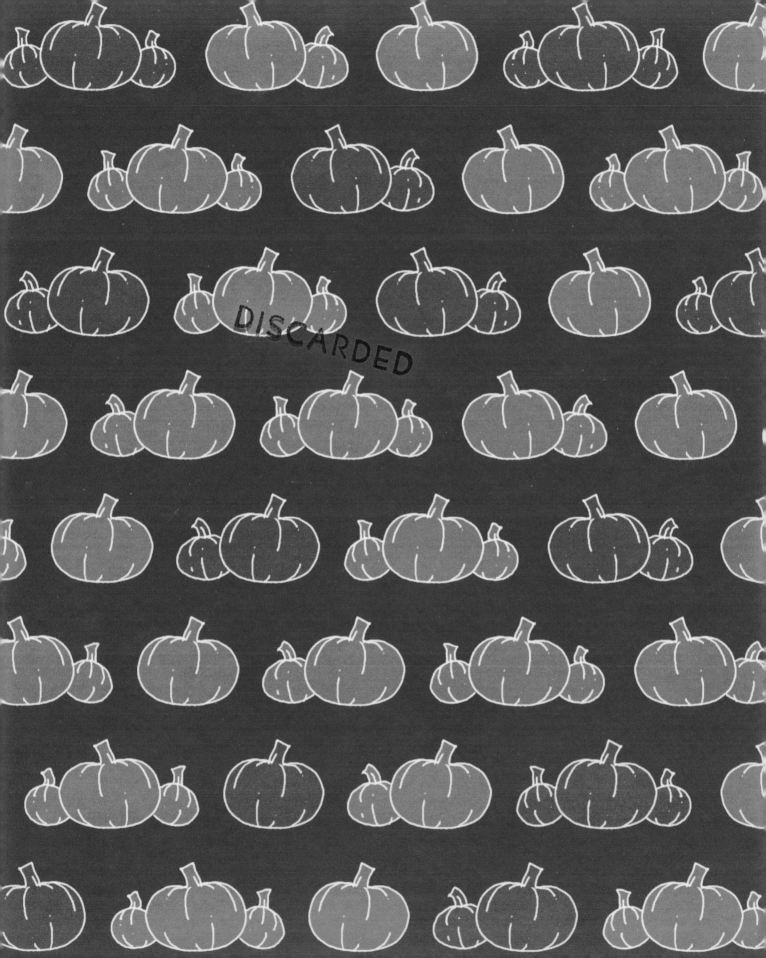